DATE DUE

Demco, Inc. 38-293

*For Oskar, Joe next door,
and Tiziana* ~ J. B.-B.

Text copyright © 1998 by Martin Waddell
Illustrations copyright © 1998 by John Bendall-Brunello

First U.S. edition 1998

Library of Congress Cataloging-in-Publication Data

Waddell, Martin.
Yum, yum, yummy / by Martin Waddell ;
illustrated by John Bendall-Brunello. — 1st U.S. ed.
p.   cm.
Summary: Greedy Guzzley Bear steals honey from three cubs,
but Mummy Bear comes to the rescue.
ISBN 0-7636-0477-1 (hardcover) — ISBN 0-7636-0479-8 (paperback)
[1. Bears—Fiction. 2. Honey—Fiction. 3. Mother and child—Fiction.]
I. Bendall-Brunello, John, ill. II. Title.
PZ7.W1137Yu   1998
[E]—dc21   97-29760

10 9 8 7 6 5 4 3 2 1

Printed in Singapore

This book was typeset in Horley.
The pictures were done in pencil and watercolor.

Candlewick Press
2067 Massachusetts Avenue
Cambridge, Massachusetts 02140

Yum, Yum, Yummy

Martin Waddell

illustrated by

John Bendall-Brunello

CANDLEWICK PRESS
CAMBRIDGE, MASSACHUSETTS

One day three little bears went off to the Honeybee Tree to get honey for Mummy.

Guzzley was there,
but the three little bears
didn't see Guzzley Bear.

The three little
bears filled their
pots with honey.
Then they set off
for home.

Greedy Guzzley was there,
but the three little bears
didn't see Guzzley Bear.

"Grr-grr-grr!"
growled Guzzley Bear.
"Give me your honey!"

Yum, yum, yummy!

The honey went into Guzzley's big tummy.

Three scared little bears ran
all the way home.
"Guzzley Bear stole our honey,"
they told their mummy.
"Don't be scared, little bears,"
said Mummy. "You go back
for more honey. I'll see to
that old Guzzley Bear."

The three little bears went back to the Honeybee Tree. Guzzley Bear crept up behind them. Mummy was there but Guzzley Bear didn't see Mummy Bear.

"**Grr-grr-grr!**"
growled Guzzley Bear.
"Give me your honey!"
But out of the
bushes came . . .

Mummy!

Guzzley Bear never
came back anymore. The
honey went into three
little bear tummies . . .

and Mummy's.
Yum,
yum,
yum,
yummy!